Oliver Optic

The Picnic Party

A Story for Little Folks

Oliver Optic

The Picnic Party
A Story for Little Folks

ISBN/EAN: 9783743427471

Manufactured in Europe, USA, Canada, Australia, Japa

Cover: Foto ©Andreas Hilbeck / pixelio.de

Manufactured and distributed by brebook publishing software
(www.brebook.com)

Oliver Optic

The Picnic Party

THE PICNIC PARTY.

I.

DURING the summer vacation, one year, Josephine and Edward Brown spent a month with Flora Lee and her brother. The visitors were distant relations, and lived in the city of New York.

Josephine was a pretty little girl, but she had a very bad habit which made for her a great many enemies. It is a common fault, not only among children, but among grown-up people, and which often makes others dislike them.

My readers shall see this fault for themselves, as the story advances, and I hope they will understand and avoid it.

Perhaps Josephine was not so much to blame as her parents for this bad habit. I am sure she did not understand, and did not know, why her companions soon took a dislike to her.

Josephine and Edward were very much pleased with the home of Mr. Lee, and for several days they were as happy as the days were long. They were not used to the country,

and it seemed to them just as though they should never be tired of running in the fields, and of visiting the woods and the river.

One day, after they had been playing very hard in the orchard, the children all went into the house to rest themselves. Josephine threw herself upon the sofa in the sitting room, and said she was tired almost to death.

Of course she did not mean so, and only intended to say that she was very tired, though I think it likely that, if an excursion to the woods or the river had been proposed, she would not have been too tired to join the party.

"Won't you please to bring me a glass of water, Flora?" said Josephine, after she had rested a little while.

"To be sure I will," replied

Flora, rising, and getting the glass of water for her friend.

"Thank you," added Josephine, as she took the glass, and drank its contents.

Flora, when she had given her the water, happened to think of something in the entry which she wanted, and went for it.

"Won't you please to take this tumbler, Frank?" said Josephine.

Frank did not make any reply, but rose from his seat, took the glass, and put it upon the table.

"Thank you, Frank; I never was so tired in all my life."

"Are you quite sure of that?"

"Quite sure."

"I am sorry for it," replied Frank, rather dryly.

"Why are you so sorry?"

"Edward and I are going

fishing; and father said Flora might go with us."

"That will be nice," exclaimed Josephine, jumping up from the sofa, as fresh as though she had just got out of bed. "I will go too."

"You?" said Frank, laughing.

"Why shouldn't I go? You know I like to go to the river above all things. Won't we have a nice time!"

"*We* will, I think."

"Don't you mean to let me go? Come, now, I think you · are real rude, Frank," pouted the young lady from New York.

"Let you go? I am sure I shall not prevent you from going."

"What do you mean, then?"

"Didn't you say just now that you were tired almost to death? that you were never so tired in your life before?"

"I was; but I feel rested now."

"You got over it very quick."

"Are you going, Josey?" asked Flora, as she returned to the room.

"To be sure, I am."

"Well, we are all ready. It is ten o'clock now, and father said John might go with us at that time," said Frank, moving towards the door.

"I am ready," replied Flora, who had brought her rubbers in from the entry.

· "So am I," said Josephine. "Dear me! my rubbers are up in my chamber. Won't you go up and get them for me, Flora?"

Flora went up stairs and got the rubbers for her, and Josephine thanked her for her kindness. The boys were waiting in front of the house with their fish poles on their shoulders, by this time, and, as boys always are when they are going fishing, were very much in a hurry.

"O, dear me!" exclaimed Josephine, when she had put on her rubbers. "I left my sack in the orchard. Please to go and get it for me, Flora, and I will make Frank wait for us till you return with it."

"Yes, I will get it;" and she bounded away for the missing garment.

"We never shall get to the river at this rate," said Edward, when his sister had told him the cause of the new delay. It all comes of having girls go with us."

"There is time enough, Master Edward," added John,

the young man who worked in the garden and helped take care of the horses. "You will be tired enough before dinner time."

"Here comes Flora. She is a dear good girl. I am very much obliged to you," said Josephine, as she took the sack. "Now I will be ever so much more obliged to you if you will go into the house and get me one of those nice doughnuts, such as we had for supper last night. I am almost starved."

"I think you had better not go a-fishing then," added Edward, bluntly.

"Why not? Can't I be hungry and go a-fishing?"

"We don't want to wait all day for you."

In a few minutes Flora joined them again; but the poor girl was sweating, and out of breath, she had run so fast in supplying the wants of her little New York friend.

"I believe we are all ready now," said Josephine, as she took the doughnut and began to nibble at it, just as a mouse nibbles at a piece of cheese.

"If you are not, we will go without you," replied Edward, whose patience, as the reader has seen, was by no means

proof against his sister's repeated delays.

"There! as true as I'm
alive, there is one thing more.
I have forgotten my sun-
shade," exclaimed Josephine.

"Never mind your sun-
shade. What do you want
of a sunshade when you are
going a-fishing?" said Edward, as he moved down the
path towards the road.

"O, I can't go without my

sunshade. I should be as brown as an Indian before we got back."

" No matter if you are. Come along, or else stay at home, and not bother us any longer."

" Please, Flora, won't you go up in my room and get it for me? I will do as much for you any time. And we will walk along, and you can overtake us before we

have gone far.   We will walk
slowly."

It is very likely that Flora
thought her young friend was
imposing upon her; but without making any reply, she ran
for the sunshade.   She had
to look in quite a number
of places before she found it,
for Josephine could not always tell where she had left
her things; and when Flora
overtook the party, she was

so weary and out of breath
that she did not enjoy the
rest of the walk very much.

Do not my readers see
by this time what Josephine's
fault was?

The Lame Girl.

II.

I DO not know how many fish the boys caught, but I do know that Flora almost wished she had staid at home, for when she got to the river she was so tired she could hardly stand.

Flora could not help feeling that it was not kind of her friend to ask so much of

her. She was not her mis-
tress, and was just as able to
wait upon herself as Flora
was to wait upon her.

Yet she was patient and
kind, and did not quarrel with
her. Josephine was always
polite when she asked these
favors, and always thanked
her when she had done them.
Perhaps this made the matter a little better, though I
think her politeness was cun-

ning rather than kindness of heart.

I have another story to tell of Josephine and her friends, which will still further illustrate her fault, and show how she was cured of it.

A few days after the fishing excursion, Flora's mother said she might have a picnic party in the woods on the other side of the river. To add to the pleasure of the occasion, Mr. Lee had a tent put up in the woods, and erected a swing for the children.

The boys and girls were delighted with the plan, and Flora and Frank invited all the children in the neighborhood to join the party.

They were to start at nine o'clock, or as soon as the dew was off the grass. The distance to the woods was about

a mile, and the children said
they would much rather walk,
though Mr. Lee offered to
carry them over in a large
hay wagon.

There was one little girl
who was too lame to walk
this distance, and Frank said
he would draw her in his
little wagon.   To divide the
load, and add to the pleasure of all, he fastened a long
rope to the pole of the wagon,

and all the boys, about fifteen in number, were to take hold of the rope, just as men draw an engine.

At nine o'clock the happy party had collected in front of Mr. Lee's house, each one having a little basket of provisions which were to furnish the noonday feast in the grove.

"Well, Josey, are you all ready?" asked Flora, very

pleasantly, as the clock struck nine.

"Yes, I think I am. Let me see. Dear me, no; I left my gloves up stairs. Won't you go up and get them for me, Flora?" replied Josephine.

"Is there any thing else you will want?" asked Flora, for she could not help thinking that her friend had made her run up and down stairs half a dozen times on similar occasions.

"No, I guess not, Flora."

But no sooner had Flora returned with the gloves, than Josephine thought of something else. After a while, however, she got every thing, and the party started for the woods.

The boys led the procession, drawing the wagon after them. Frank and Edward had the pole, and they were very careful lest the little lame girl should be upset and hurt.

The girls at once followed, and when they had gone a little way, Flora thought it would be nice to sing one of their school songs. So they went singing on their way, as happy as the larks in the morning.

"What fine apples!" exclaimed Josephine, as the party were passing Mr. Lee's orchard.

"They are very fine looking apples, but they are not ripe," replied Katy Green, who was walking near her.

"I think they must be ripe. They look good, at any rate. Won't you be so kind as to get me one of them?"

"They will make you sick if you eat them," said Katy.

" O, no, they won't.   If you will get me one, I will be very much obliged to you."

Even Katy Green, who was not very well acquainted with the New York miss, could not resist this appeal, and she accordingly climbed over the fence and got two or three of the apples which she found on the ground.

As Katy had said, the apples were not fit to eat, and

they were thrown away. They had gone but a little farther before Josephine saw some more apples, which looked very nice.

"I am sure those apples are ripe. See how red they are. I know they are ripe," said she.

"Those are Baldwin apples. They are not fit to eat till winter comes," replied Katy.

"I am sure they must be

ripe. I have eaten just such apples as those in New York in the summer. Will you be so kind as to get me one?"

"They are not ripe, I tell you," answered Katy, impatiently. "I have known the tree for ever so many years, and I know just as well as any thing can be that they are not ripe."

"But won't you be kind enough to get me one of

them ? " persisted Miss Josephine.

" If you want one you may get it yourself," said Katy.

" How very rude you are ! " replied Josephine.

" Rude ? " sneered Katy. " Do you suppose I want to climb over that fence for nothing ? "

" It isn't such a very dreadful thing to climb over that fence."

"Then why don't you do it yourself?"

"You are used to things of the kind, and I am not."

"If you want green apples, that are of no use to any one, you had better get used to climbing fences, for I shall not do it for you any more."

Josephine declared that this speech was very rude indeed; and perhaps it was; but it was plain common sense. The little New York lady was so angry that she left Katy, and went to walk with Jenny Brown.

After the party had crossed the bridge, the boys took down the bars by the side of the road, and they entered the woods. There was a fine smooth road leading for several miles through the forest, and the children enjoyed the walk very much.

Every few moments Josephine saw something which she wanted, and instead of trying to get it herself, as she should have done, she asked somebody to bring it for her.

In one place she saw some checkerberry plants growing; and, at her request, Jenny picked her a handful of them. Then she wanted a swamp pink, which Jenny also procured for her.

But Josephine's wants were so many, that Jenny soon got tired of supplying them; and she was obliged to ask some one else to wait upon her.

One after another, her companions got tired of her, and either refused to wait upon her, or left her. She would have called upon Flora, but she walked by the side of the lame girl, and was busy talking with her.

Josephine wanted but very few of the things which she asked others to get for her. She had a habit of *wanting* all the time, and did not seem to be easy unless some one was waiting upon her.

At home, her father had plenty of servants, and she did not realize that her friends and companions had any thing to think of besides her comfort. But even servants should be treated with kindness, and children should not call upon them, or others, to do for them what they can just as well do themselves.

In the Woods.

III.

WHEN the party reached the picnic ground, Josephine had more wants than ever. She called upon this one to bring her a mug of water, and upon that one to get her a dough-nut; upon one to hold her shawl while she arranged her dress, and another to take off her rubbers.

If she had been a queen, and all the rest of the children her servants, she could not have been more free in her use of them. Before they had been in the woods a single hour, almost all her companions disliked her greatly, and tried to avoid her.

She was selfish, and wanted to use the swing all the time. When she had swung four times as long as any of the rest of the party, she thought it was "very rude" of them when they said she must get out, for they would not swing her another time.

After dinner, some of the girls said they were going to get some oak leaves to make chaplets for their heads.

"Where are you going?" asked Josephine.

"O, into the woods, ever so far," replied Jenny, who

did not want her to go with them.

"I will go, too," said Josephine.

"It is as much as half a mile to the place," added Jenny; "and I am afraid you will get very tired."

"I think I can stand it as well as the others."

"We are used to running in the woods, and you are a city girl, you know."

"I want to go very much."

"We don't want you to go," said Katy Green, bluntly.

"That's very rude of you to say so," replied Josephine. "I don't see why I shouldn't go, if I wish."

"You can go, if you will only wait upon yourself," said Jenny.

"Wait upon myself? How very rude that is! I'm sure I've only asked you to do one or two little favors for me, and you call that waiting upon me."

"Don't be unkind to her, girls," said Flora.

"*She* doesn't call it waiting upon me when she does a little favor for me. I am sure I am willing to do as much for you as you do for me."

"Let her go with you, girls —won't you?" said Flora.

For Flora's sake they consented, though they did not like to have her with them.

" But how shall we bring the leaves ? " asked Jenny. " We shall want as many as a bushel of them, for we must all go home with crowns on our heads."

" I'll tell you what we can do," added Katy. " We can take the little wagon. That will hold a bushel."

" So we can; and it will hold

more than a bushel. Come along; we are all ready."

Katy and Jenny were the two girls who were going for the leaves, and one of them took hold of each side of the pole of the wagon. They started off at a brisk pace, Josephine following behind the wagon.

"Pray, don't go so fast; I can't keep up with you if you do," said the New York miss.

"I can't help it. You may go back if you can't. We are in a hurry. We shall not get our chaplets made till dark if we don't make haste with the leaves."

Josephine was obliged to quicken her pace, or be left behind; but she complained a great deal of the rudeness of the girls in walking so fast.

After they had gone some distance, she saw some curious leaves, and she wanted a few of them. She said, half a dozen times, she wished she had some, and finally asked Katy if she wouldn't be so very kind as to get her a few of them.

"Yes, I'll get them," said Katy; and in a moment she had procured some of the curious leaves and given them to Josephine.

"Thank you, thank you;

I am very much obliged to you," said she, as she took the leaves.

"Yes; but I want something more than 'thank you,'" replied Katy.

"Well, what do you want?" asked Josephine, not a little surprised at the answer she had received.

"You said you were willing to do as much for us as we did for you. Did you mean so?"

"Well, I suppose I did."

"We will be fair with you —won't we, Jenny?"

"To be sure we will."

"Well, it is no more than fair that you should take turns with us in drawing the wagon. So you may take hold of the pole, and make yourself useful."

"I can't."

"Won't you be so very kind as to help draw the wagon?"

said Katy, imitating the polite tones of the New York miss.

"I can't draw it. I am not strong enough to do such hard work."

"You can try it, at least; and when you get tired I will take your place."

"I would rather not, if you please."

"But I had much rather you would, if you please."

"Really, I cannot."

"But, really, you must."

"I could not do such a thing as draw that wagon."

"You must try; if you don't, we will run away and leave you."

Josephine thought this was more rude than any thing else they had done; but there was no escape, and she took her place at the pole of the wagon.

Before they had gone ten

rods, she declared she could draw the wagon no farther, if they killed her for refusing. Katy took her place then, and pretty soon they left the road, and went into the thick forest, to a place where there was plenty of oak leaves growing near the ground.

When they reached the spot, Josephine sat down on a rock. Her companions tried to make her help them pick the leaves;

but she said she was so tired she could not possibly do any thing.

In a very short time the body of the wagon was filled with leaves, and the girls were ready to return to the picnic grounds.

"We are going, Josephine; are you ready?" asked Jenny.

"I can't go yet. I am tired almost to death."

"We told you you would

be; but you would come," said Katy.

"I didn't think it was so far."

"We told you how far it was. We have been here ever so many times before, and know all about it. Come, quick."

"I don't feel able to walk back," sighed Josephine.

"Don't you, indeed?"

"I am sure I can't."

"What are you going to do — stay here all night?"

"Couldn't you draw me back on the wagon? There is room enough for me on top of the leaves."

The girls made no reply; but both of them laughed as though something very funny had happened.

"What are you laughing at?"

"Do you think we are going to drag a great girl like you back to the grounds? I guess not," replied Katy.

"I should think you might."

"We don't like you well enough to do that," said Katy; and then both of the girls laughed again.

"You needn't laugh at me," said Josephine, beginning to cry.

"O, you needn't cry; we didn't hurt you any. But

come along, if you are coming. We can't wait here any longer."

"I can't walk back. You *must* draw me back in the wagon," sobbed Josephine.

"We shall do nothing of the kind."

"Yes, you shall. If you don't, I will tell Mr. Lee."

"Do, if you like."

"I will stay here, then, if you won't drag me. What

will you tell Flora when she asks for me?"

"Tell her where you are, of course."

Josephine did not believe they would go away and leave her there alone. She thought they would return in a little while, and consent to draw her in the wagon; so she let them go.

She sat on the rock and cried till she had got tired

of crying, and then finding her companions did not return, she got up and tried to find her way to the road.

Josephine and the Partridge.

IV.

JOSEPHINE was not used to the woods, and she did not know which way to go to find the road. She had paid no heed to the path by which she had reached the place where the leaves were obtained.

She had been so vexed and angry, because her companions would not let her ride, that she had not even looked to see which way they went when they left her.

She sat on a stump and cried till she was tired of crying, and till she found it would not get her out of the woods. Then she got up, and looked around her; but she could not tell in what direction the road lay from her. She listened, and could hear no sound. It was plain that

Katy and Jenny had left her alone.

The solemn stillness of the forest awed her, and she was afraid to stay there, with no human being near her.   Once a cat-bird uttered a terrible scream, and Josephine had nearly 'fainted with terror.

She thought it must be some awful monster to make such a hideous noise, and as soon as she was able to do so, she ran away from the spot as fast as her feet would carry her.

As she hastened through the bushes, and over the dry leaves, a partridge, alarmed by her presence, rose from the ground, and flew away, making a whirring noise with his wings that made Josephine scream with terror.

The poor girl wandered about for two hours in the

woods, till she was so tired
she could walk no longer.
She thought of the Children
in the Woods, and others who
had been left in the forest,
and she was afraid she should
never see her friends again.

I think she was more fright-
ened than hurt, for there was
nothing in the woods that was
disposed to injure her. The
cat-birds, the partridges, and
even the snakes, if there were

any there, were more afraid of her than she was of them. If they saw her, they would run away as fast as they could.

Josephine sat down upon a log, and wished she had not been so angry and stubborn. She even thought it was not fair of her to ask the girls to draw her in the wagon.

While she was thinking of what she had done, and wondering what would become of her, she heard footsteps in the distance, and presently one of the boys shouted her name with all his might.

"Here I am," replied Josephine, getting up and walking in the direction from which the sound had come.

In a moment she saw Frank Lee; and pretty soon half a dozen of the boys came up to the place.

"Where have you been, Josephine? We have been looking for you for more than an hour."

"I have been trying to find my way to the road."

"You are ever so far from the road," said Frank. "Why didn't you go back with the girls?"

"They wouldn't let me ride on the wagon."

"Wouldn't they?" added

her brother, who was one of the party. "That was too bad, Josey, for you to ask them to drag you."

"I was so tired that I did not feel able to walk," replied Josephine, who wanted to give the best excuse she could.

"We won't stop to talk about it now," added Frank. "Father and mother have come, and you can tell them all about it, Josephine."

The boys led the way back to the picnic grounds; but Josephine was so tired she could hardly get back; and when she joined the party, she was completely worn out by the fatigue and anxiety of her lonely walk.

Neither Mr. nor Mrs. Lee said any thing about the matter till they got home. They came in the carryall, and Josephine rode back. The rest of the children walked home, singing like larks all the way.

"You got lost in the woods, — did you, Josephine?" said Mrs. Lee, in the evening.

"Yes, ma'am. Those rude girls left me alone, when they knew I could not find the way back," replied Josephine, who wished to make her side of the question appear as well as she could.

"Is that the whole story, my

child?" asked Mrs. Lee, with a smile.

"I wanted them to draw me in the wagon, and they wouldn't."

"Wasn't that asking rather too much of them?"

"I don't know but it was; but they needn't have left me there all alone."

"What could they have done?"

"I think they needn't have

left me," repeated Josephine, not very pleasantly.

"You insisted on going with them, though they told you they were going a long distance, and you would be very tired. I don't think you can reasonably blame them."

"They knew I wasn't used to the woods."

"You told them that you wouldn't go with them unless they drew you on the wagon.

You might have followed them without any difficulty."

"I didn't think they would leave me."

"I don't know what else they could do. You would not go with them; and the least they could do was to let you have your own way."

"I won't go with them again," pouted Josephine.

"They did not want you to go with them. It was only at

Flora's request that they consented you should go. Josephine, you have got a bad habit, which I hope you will cure before long."

" A bad habit, ma'am ? " said Josephine, looking up at Mrs. Lee, as though she thought it very strange that she should have a bad habit.

" Yes, my child. I noticed it when you first came here. It has made you very unpopular with your playmates. When I went to the picnic this afternoon, I found that nearly all the girls were glad you had left them. They all said Katy and Jenny had done just right in leaving you."

"It was very rude of them," said Josephine, beginning to cry. "I haven't done any thing to make them hate me so."

"I hope they don't *hate* you, but they don't like you. I do not wonder that they don't like you, either. You may call it rude, but the girls can never like you while you try to make servants of them."

"Why, Mrs. Lee!" exclaimed Josephine.

"You may be surprised, but I have seen you send Flora upon a dozen errands in half an hour."

"I have asked her to do something for me very often, perhaps; but I only asked it as a favor."

"One should not ask too many favors. Now let me give you a rule, which I hope you will follow. *Never ask others to do for you what you can just as well do yourself.* You will have to ask many favors of your friends; and they will most cheerfully confer them, if you do not ask too many."

"The girls said I was always asking them to do something for me. But I am sure I did not mean any thing wrong, and I will try to do better."

"You are very polite to your playmates," added Mrs. Lee; "and politeness is a good thing in a little girl; but we should be sure that it is true politeness, for there are two kinds."

"I never knew there was more than one kind of politeness," said Josephine.

"There are two kinds: one which comes from a kind heart, and which is a desire to promote the happiness of others. The other kind is nothing but cunning — such as the fox practises when he wants to catch a chicken. It is selfish — put on to make others do as you wish them to do. I am afraid your politeness was somewhat of the latter kind."

"I am glad to know it, and I will try to do better."

And she did try to do better. Though she did not at first succeed, her friends saw that she was trying to improve, and they were very kind and very indulgent to

her; so that before she returned to New York, she was
liked as well as any other little girl in Riverdale.

www.ingramcontent.com/pod-product-compliance
Lightning Source LLC
Chambersburg PA
CBHW022014050726
47499CB00007BA/2574